My Mama Sings

by *Jeanne Whitehouse Peterson*

illustrated by Sandra Speidel

HarperCollins*Publishers*

To my mother, who always listens,
and to my daughters, who help me sing
—J.W.P.

To my daughter, Zoe, who keeps me
singing, and to my good friends,
Brandon Taylor and Wanda Lollis
—S.S.

MY MAMA SINGS
Text copyright © 1994 by Jeanne Whitehouse Peterson
Illustrations copyright © 1994 by Sandra Speidel
Printed in the U.S.A. All rights reserved.

Library of Congress Cataloging-in-Publication Data
Peterson, Jeanne Whitehouse.
    My mama sings / by Jeanne Whitehouse Peterson ; illustrated by
Sandra Speidel.
        p.   cm.
    Summary: Mama has special old songs for all occasions, until the
time comes when she has no song ready and her little boy supplies
one.
    ISBN 0-06-023854-2. — ISBN 0-06-023859-3 (lib. bdg.)
    |1. Mothers and sons—Fiction.   2. Singing—Fiction.
3. Afro-Americans—Fiction.| I. Speidel, Sandra, ill.   II. Title.
PZ7.P4444My   1994   91-72
|E|—dc20   CIP
                                                                 AC

Typography by Elynn Cohen
1   2   3   4   5   6   7   8   9   10
❖
First Edition

Also by Jeanne Whitehouse Peterson

I Have a Sister, My Sister Is Deaf
Sometimes I Dream Horses
While the Moon Shines Bright

My mama sings me no new songs.
We get along with used tunes
from the radio,
and hymns she learned
with the Harmony Choir.

She has one song for when daffodils
are blooming, and winter is over,
and everything's turning
green, green, green—

And one for hot, hot summer nights
when I'm too sticky to sleep.

Then my mama sings me
the same soft blues
her mama taught her.

Low and slow,
the wavery tune
smooths the warm sheets
in my tiny room.

When we stamp our way
through piles of dry leaves,
my mama always makes a clicking rhythm
with the tip of her tongue.

"Is that a cricket song?" I ask.
"Yes," Mama nods. "I learned it
from Grandpa when I was young."

And, when snow blows
over the tops of our boots,
Mama always whistles
the same clear tune.

Later, we have a chocolate party.
I invite Pam and Ammo and Nigel.
Mama finds her scratchy dancing records
and begins to pop corn by the fire.

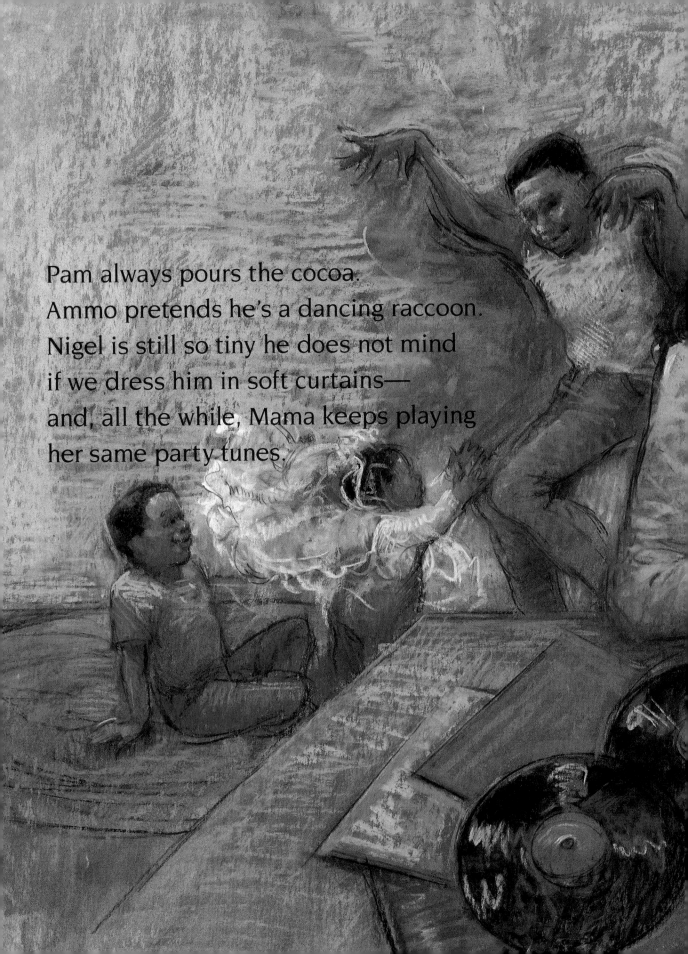

Pam always pours the cocoa.
Ammo pretends he's a dancing raccoon.
Nigel is still so tiny he does not mind
if we dress him in soft curtains—
and, all the while, Mama keeps playing
her same party tunes.

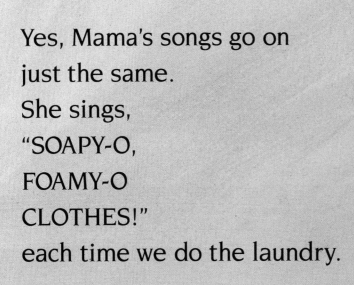

Yes, Mama's songs go on
just the same.
She sings,
"SOAPY-O,
FOAMY-O
CLOTHES!"
each time we do the laundry.

And, on days when slow rain
drips from our windows,
Mama always sings
her loudest sunshine chant.

Mama says, "Great-aunt Gretna taught me
to sing this way."
We both laugh, because Great-aunt Gretna
is our black-and-white cat.

My mama always kids me like that.

But one morning
the car won't start,
and the bus is late,
and Mama's boss is so angry
he sends her away.

When Mama comes home
she has no songs for me.
Great-aunt Gretna and I
make our own supper.

We watch TV alone,
then wait at the window
to see the moon rise.

By myself I try singing
all of Mama's old songs,
but they don't sound the same.
So
I make up a song—
a special song for Mama—
for some other night
when she is fresh and new.

"Come Mama," I sing.
"Come with Pam and me
and Ammo and Nigel
on a trip down the street
for an ice cream treat
and a long, cool ride
on a rainbow slide."

Then I pretend that on the way home
Mama squeezes my fingers.
She calls Great-aunt Gretna
to meet us.
We make our supper
of corn bread and peaches.
We tell each other stories
we heard a long time ago.

Just before I fall asleep,
I hear Mama washing dishes.
Between *swish-swish* and *rattle-clatter*
Mama's song begins to rise
like a floating bubble.
Her voice holds me close and warm.

Suddenly, I hear Mama sing,
"Yes, I'll come down the street
for an ice cream treat
and a long, cool ride
on a rainbow slide."

Running to her I ask,
"Did you make up a new tune?"
"No," Mama laughs,
like I hoped she would.
"Today I couldn't sing
because I was blue.
This happy song
I learned from *you."*

Yes, my mama sings me no new songs.
We get along with all our used tunes
and loud sunshine chants.
But, sometimes,
Mama hears me singing my new song
and she sings it back.
Mama, Great-aunt Gretna
and I
like it like that.